THE RED SCARF

ANNE VILLENEUVE

TUNDRA BOOKS

For Mrs. Paoli and Mr. Psitorio,

Originally published in French as *L'Echarpe Rouge* by les éditions Les 400 coups, Montreal, 1999
First published in this edition by Tundra Books, Toronto, 2010

Illustrations copyright © 1999 by Anne Villeneuve
English language translation by Tundra Books, 2010

Published in Canada by Tundra Books,
75 Sherbourne Street, Toronto, Ontario M5A 2P9

Published in the United States by Tundra Books of Northern New York,
P.O. Box 1030, Plattsburgh, New York 12901

Library of Congress Control Number: 2009929064

LIBRARY AND ARCHIVES CANADA CATALOGUING IN PUBLICATION

Villeneuve, Anne
[Écharpe rouge. English]
     The red scarf / Anne Villeneuve.

Translation of: L'écharpe rouge.
ISBN 978-0-88776-989-4

     I. Title. II. Title: Écharpe rouge. English.

PS8593.I3996E2813 2010   jC843'.54   C2009-903207-4

We acknowledge the financial support of the Government of Canada through the Book Publishing Industry Development Program and that of the Government of Ontario through the Ontario Media Development Corporation's Ontario Book Initiative. We further acknowledge the support of the Canada Council for the Arts and the Ontario Arts Council for our publishing program.

ONTARIO ARTS COUNCIL
CONSEIL DES ARTS DE L'ONTARIO

Printed in China

1 2 3 4 5 6   15 14 13 12 11 10

and for Christian...

THE RED SCARF

ANNE VILLENEUVE

"Another gray day," says

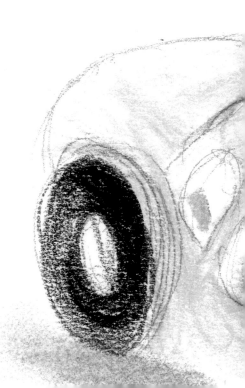

Turpin, the taxi driver.

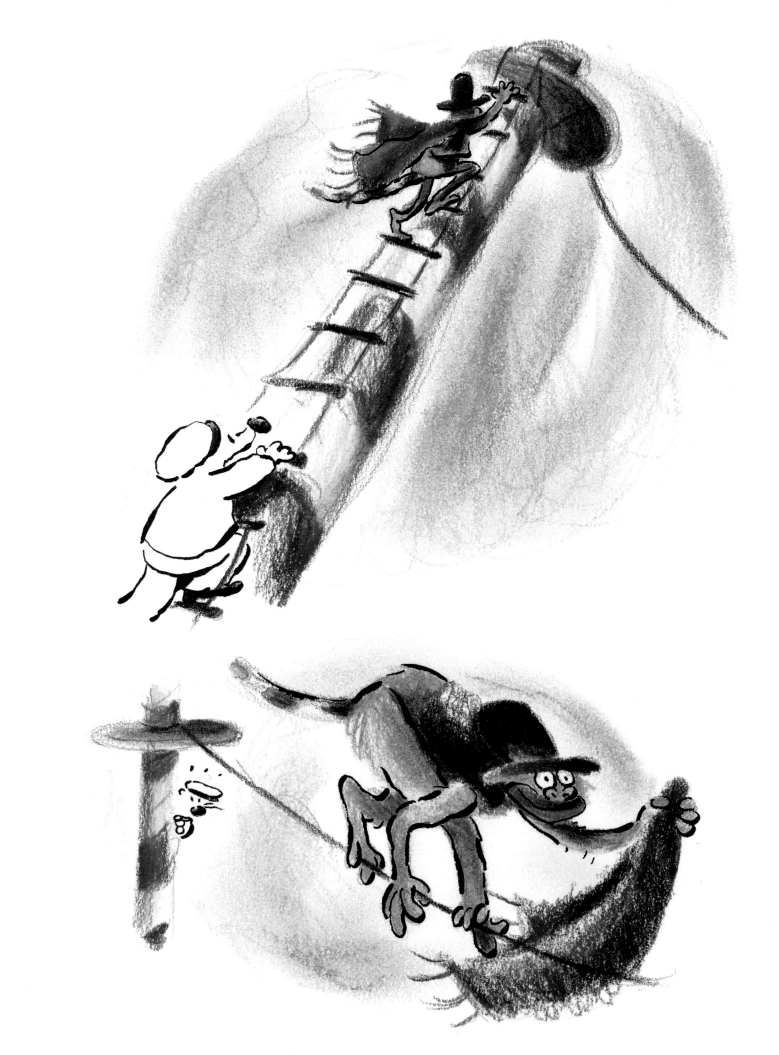

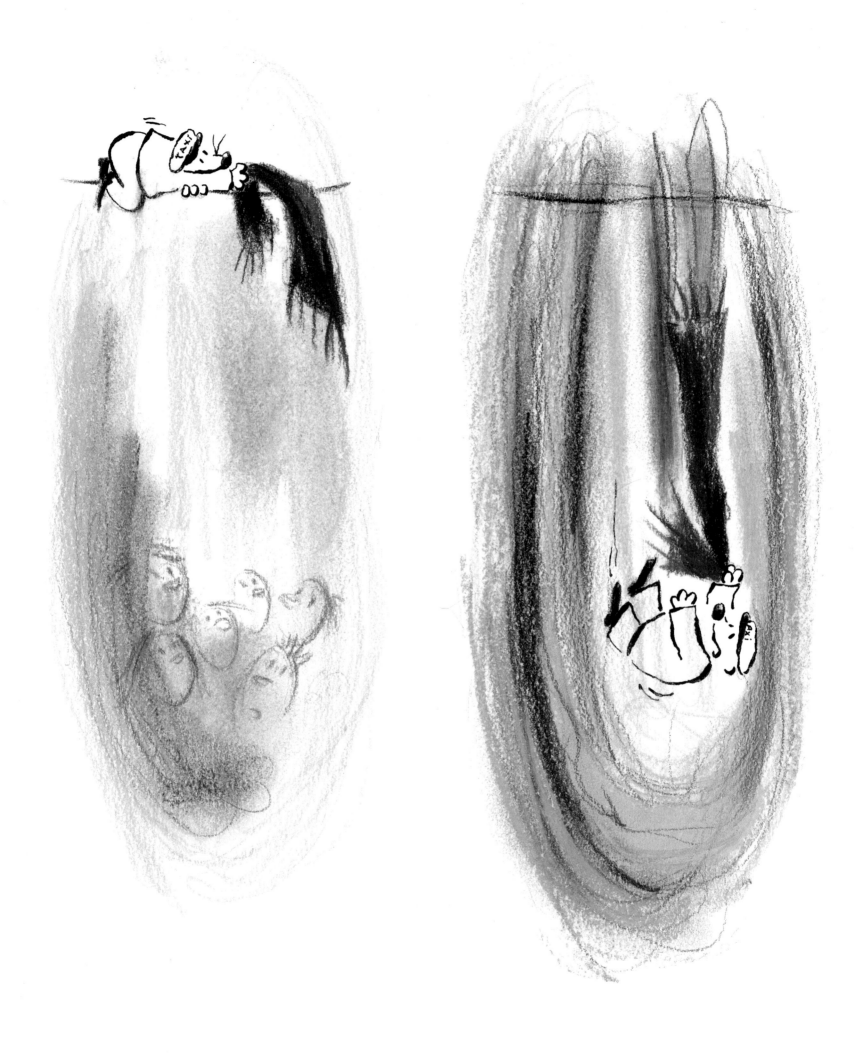